Little Blossom Stories

Jump in the Pool

By Cecilia Minden

2 Dan is at the big pool.

Dan likes to swim with his pals. 3

4

Ben jumps in the big pool.

Tim jumps in the big pool.

6 Dan stands by the big pool.

Dan looks at his pals in the big pool.

8 Ben calls, "You can do it, Dan!"

Tim calls, "You can do it, Dan!"

Dan looks at the big pool.

Dan steps back.

Dan jumps in the big pool!

Dan likes to swim with his pals.

Word List

sight words

by	his	looks	to	you
do	is	pool	wants	
does	likes	the	with	

short a words	short e words	short i words	short u words
at	Ben	big	jumps
back	steps	in	
calls		it	
can		swim	
Dan		Tim	
pals			
stands			

76 Words

Dan is at the big pool.

Dan likes to swim with his pals.

Ben jumps in the big pool.

Tim jumps in the big pool.

Dan stands by the big pool.

Dan looks at his pals in the big pool.

Ben calls, "You can do it, Dan!"

Tim calls, "You can do it, Dan!"

Dan looks at the big pool.

Dan steps back.

Dan jumps in the big pool!

Dan likes to swim with his pals.

Published in the United States of America by Cherry Lake Publishing
Ann Arbor, Michigan
www.cherrylakepublishing.com

Illustrator: Sharon Sordo

Cherry Blossom Press is an imprint of Cherry Lake Publishing.

Library of Congress Cataloging-in-Publication Data has been filed and is available at catalog.loc.gov

Printed in the United States of America
Corporate Graphics

Cecilia Minden is the former director of the Language and Literacy Program at Harvard Graduate School of Education.
She earned her PhD in Reading Education at the University of Virginia. Dr. Minden has written extensively for early readers.
She is passionate about matching children to the very book they need to improve their skills and progress to a deeper
understanding of all the wonder books can hold. Dr. Minden and her family live in McKinney, Texas.